For Darrin, my youngest oldest friend — MV
For Christopher, David and Nicholas — KN

Printed by permission of Margaret Hamilton Books Pty Ltd., Australia
First Canadian edition published 1994
Text copyright © 1993 by Marcia Vaughan   Illustrations copyright © 1993 by Kilmeny Niland

Canadian Cataloguing in Publication Data
Vaughan, Marcia K
Sheep shape

ISBN 1-55074-207-8

1. Sheep – Juvenile fiction. I. Niland, Kilmeny. II. Title.
PZ7.V452Sh 1994   j823   C93-095410-6

Kids Can Press Ltd., 29 Birch Avenue, Toronto, Ontario, Canada, M4V 1E2
Typeset in 22/30pt Gill Sans. **Produced in Hong Kong by Mandarin Offset.**

Marcia Vaughan and Kilmeny Niland

Kids Can Press Ltd.
Toronto

One day Farmer Gray got completely
carried away and sheared his sheep in shapes.

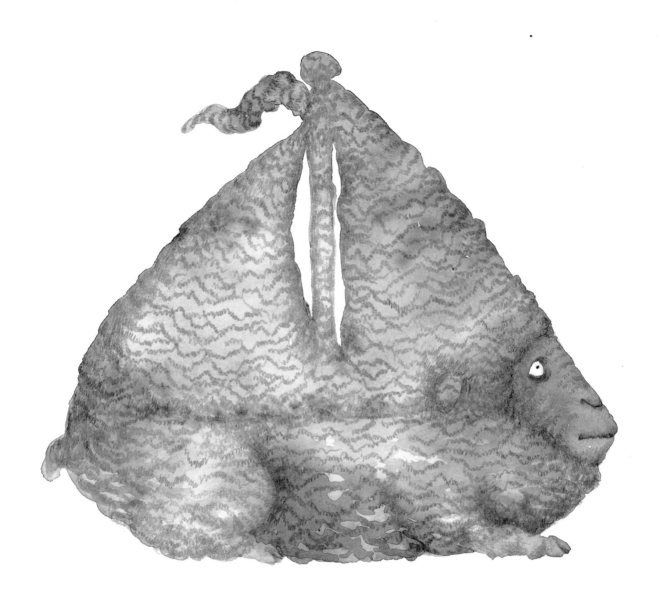

One sheep was ship shape.

One sheep was ape shape.

One sheep was a tree.

Another was a pot of tea.

There was one like a mouse.

And two like a house.

Three made a fountain.

Four made a mountain.

There was a ram shaped like jam.

And a ewe like a shoe.

A star.

A car.

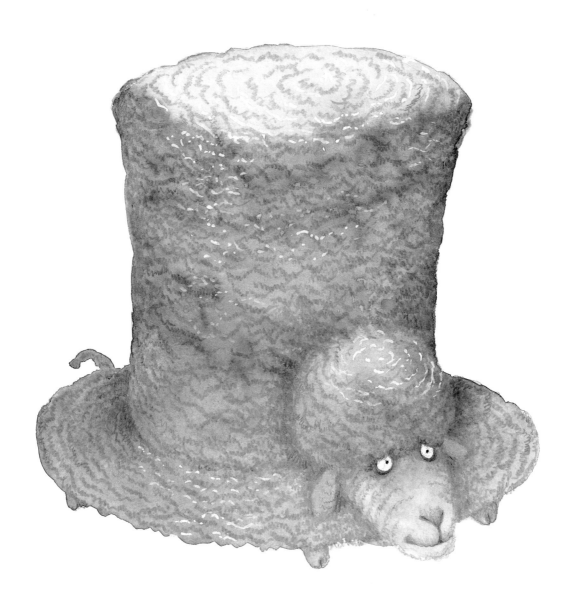

A top hat.

A door mat.

A garden snail.

A spouting whale.

A fat cat.

And a black bat.

By day's end Farmer Gray had sheared all the sheep, the cat, the dog, the hedge and his long red beard into the most remarkable shapes.

Some folks say he got a little *too* carried away.

But not Farmer Gray.
He liked it that way!